THE DIARY OF
CHICKABIDDY BABY

EMMA KALLOK

TRICYCLE PRESS
Berkeley, California

To Mordy, the tubby tabby. Thanks and love to my
friend, Jonathan London, for his help and support. To
Judy London, my former teacher, who inspired me to
write and helped me discover my talent. Love to my
mother, who has always been there. Love to my sister, my
very first editor. Love to my fabulous and supportive
grandparents, Lee and John Kallok. Thanks to Stephanie
Joseph, the best friend a girl could have!

Tricycle Press
P.O. Box 7123, Berkeley, CA 94707
www.tenspeed.com

Cover and jacket design by Jean Sanchirico
Cover and jacket illustration ©1999 by G. Brian Karas
Interior design by Toni Tajima
Map illustration on page 88 by Hannah Kallok
Text set in Stone Serif, Stone Sans, Kidprint, Times Roman, and
Helvetica. Cover set in Berliner.

Library of Congress Cataloging-in-Publication Data
Kallok, Emma.
   The diary of Chickabiddy Baby / Emma Kallok.
      p. cm.
   Summary: Eleven-year-old Prudence keeps a diary of her summer vacation,
which is filled with first crushes, squabbles with friends, and a secret admirer.
   ISBN 1-883672-90-2 (alk. paper)
   ISBN 10883672-87-2 (cloth)
   I. Title.   PZ7.K11747 Di 1999
   [Fic]—dc21   99-11744
                                                                       CIP

First printing, 1999
Printed in Canada
   2 3 4 5 6 — 03 02 01 00 99

Contents

1 Embarrassments 1

2 The School BBQ 5

3 Worry 7

4 The Sunfellows 8

5 Mither 10

6 Cholesterol 12

7 Religion 15

8 Pudding-Head 18

9 Hormones 22

10 The Grays 25

11 A Swimming Invitation 30

12 Up in the Clouds 33

13 Poetry 34

14 A Hangover 39

15 Mouse 41

16 The Jealousy of Jason 44

17 The Time Quilt Begins 47

18 A Bunch o' Malarkey 50

19 Dream Candles 53

20 Trouble and $18.50 58

21 Austen 61

22 The First Note 63

23 Fourth of July 65

24 The Big Idea 66

25 Singin' in the Rain 68

26 The Lake 70

27 Mackenzie 73

28 Sea Monster 76

29 Mrs. Cappuccino 78

30 White Lies 82

31 De Gabriella Cappuccino Island 86

32 Good-bye, So Soon 89

33 Welcome Home!! 91

34 Notes and Fried Chicken 94

35 The Deep, Dark Secret of
    Cathy Sunfellow 96

36 Mouse's Breakdown 99

37 Mega Love 102

38 The Discovered Lover 106

39 Fed Up!! 108

40 Too Much News 111

41 An Announcement 114

42 See Ya! 117

1 Embarrassments

Diary,

My name is Prudence Brinker. Prudence. Yuck. It reminds me of pudding. Tapioca pudding. I hate tapioca pudding, but I like chocolate pudding. My mom acts like a lunatic, and my father is a writer, so I guess you could call him a lunatic, too, and I have two brothers. My brothers are Benny and Yo-Yo. They are inseparable. Benny is six and a half and Yo-Yo is eight. His real name is Yuba, after the county, but he thinks Yo-Yo is cool, and it became his name. I am Prudence of course, and I am eleven. I am the only eleven-year-old in fourth grade because I started school late. It's June now, only one more day until school is out, June sixteenth. My friend, Marjorie, otherwise known as Mouse (because she looks like one, just don't tell her that), is going away for half of the summer.

★ ★ ★

"Pru, pass the frozen peas to me, won't you honey?" Mom said. I passed them to her and she popped them into the microwave to cook.

"Mom, could you please listen to me?" I pleaded.

"I'll give you a rain check," Mom said. She threw back her head and laughed.

"Mo-om! I mean it," I said. Deity!

Yo-Yo and Benny raced across the tile floor and clattered into the family room.

"Sorry, honey," Mom said, wringing a wet dish towel over her head to cool her forehead. It was a baking hot day, evening, actually.

"Okay, let me begin. And Mom, please don't interrupt," I said.

"Yes, Chickabiddy Baby?" Mom said in her loud voice. That's the special name she calls me. Everyone at our house has a nickname. I'm Chickabiddy Baby. Dad is the Mad Professor. You already know about Benjamin and Yuba. Mom is Sugar Pie.

I cleared my throat for the umpteenth time. I had wanted to say this for a long time, but I was afraid it would hurt Mom's feelings.

"Mom, you embarrass me sometimes," I finally blurted. The beads of water from the dish towel slid down Mom's forehead and dripped onto her lashes.

"I do? I'm sorry, baby. How?" she said. Her mouth opened in mock concern.

"I'll write it all down," I muttered. I tore out a page of paper from the phone pad. As I wrote, Mom shuffled around the kitchen singing off-key, "I'm in the mood for lo-ove...."

I hummed under my breath while I wrote:

EMBARRASSMENTS
1. You talk too loud.
2. You sing horribly.
3. You say dumb quotes.
4. You pick at your cuticles.
5. You ask weird and strange questions, in public!
6. You discuss weird things.
7. You talk with food in your mouth.
8. You shake your left foot when you are impatient.

UNFAIRNESS
1. You never yell or get mad at Benny and Yo-Yo.
2. You expect me to be in charge.

3. You treat me like a baby.

4. You only let me see PG movies.

MORE EMBARRASSMENTS

1. You and Dad kiss in public.

2. You hold hands under the table.

3. You put your hand in Dad's pocket
   and he does the same with you.

4. You guys act totally crazy!

5. You wear crummy clothing.

After I wrote the list, I taped it to the fridge door. "Mom," I said, "keep this all in mind."

2 The School BBQ

Diary,

Today was the school cookout.

School was okay. I was happy, and sad. Happy school was out, and sad I would be going to a different school and stuff like that.

At lunchtime parents started arriving with food and gifts for the teachers.

Marjorie was already gone, in South Dakota. I couldn't wait until the community pool opened.

Austen Russel, a boy who's been bugging me since second grade, came up to me and asked me if I could sit on my hair, which was braided, but still reached a little past my backside. "If I want to," I replied.

I finished my hot dog and went to try the hamburgers. Luckily Mom couldn't make it to the cookout. She had to go to a PTA meeting at the middle school.

After I downed my hamburger and corn-on-the-cob, Austen came up to me again. "Hey Pudding-Head," he said (Pudding-Head is his idea of a good nickname), "sit on your hair. For me."

"Not on your life," I replied. I looked at the replica of myself in his eyes. Suddenly I was falling face first into his chest!

Danny Peruzzo had pushed me. Austen stretched out his arms and grabbed me around the waist. He smelled strongly of...strawberries and pine. I like both smells. He gripped me tightly, even after I steadied myself. My face was mashed right below his collarbone. I wiggled a little, shifting. I was able to pull my face up and stand erect. My face was inches away from Austen's. I noticed I was slightly taller than him, about two inches. I'm mostly taller than all the boys. Mom calls it a "growth spurt."

Austen didn't let go. I saw the replica of myself again in his eyes. I looked weird, standing tall, while Austen held me, leaning against me so I wouldn't fall. It felt sort of weird, tingly. But I shoved him off. "Get off, you jerk!" I said. I ran into the girls' room.

3 Worry

Diary,

Mom was all crazy today. Her parents are coming from Florida. They moved there because my grandmother wanted to see a different place. She was sick of New York, where they lived before. They are strict and straight. My whole family isn't any religion, but they want us to have one. I haven't seen them for four years. Mom and I are picking them up from the evening train.

4 The Sunfellows

Diary,

When the Sunfellows came off the train, I knew it was them right away. They stood tall and efficiently. They held hands. Grandma Sunfellow, who asked me to call her Granny, wore a blue cardigan and a flowered dress that covered her legs to her knees. She wore clunky black shoes. She was short and squat with a pillowy bosom. A gigantic silver cross hung on her neck. Her white hair was pulled up tightly into a neat little bun knotted on the back of her head, which was so wrinkled, it reminded me of a dried up apple. Grandfather Sunfellow was tall, frail, and droopy, like a willow. His white hair was combed with his bangs swept across his forehead. His nose was beaky, his eyes large, colorless gray. He wore a brown pair of slacks and a plaid shirt and brown tie. They had luggage that made it look like they were going camping for a week. Grandfather

Sunfellow calls Grandma Sunfellow Mither, and she calls him Dither.

Mither smelled of lilac powder and zucchini. Dither smelled of sweet beeswax and freshly made crockery. I know what crockery smells like because my mother is a potter. Her brown pots are all over the house.

When we got to my house, Dad had just gotten out of the bathtub—with all his clothes on. It helps him think.

Mither looked horrified, but she just said in a voice like leaves crunching beneath feet, sort of like a rattlesnake hiss, "Life's been good to you, Bill." She looked around the house. Mom had tried her best to clean it up, but papers, brown pots, newspapers, toys, and clothing still littered the sofas and floors and shelves. Empty glasses and teacups stood on mounds of wet clay, covered in plastic wrap.

"Mither, won't you sit down? Dither, here's a sofa chair," Mom said quickly. It sounded as if she was going to cry.

Water dripped off Dad's wrinkled wet slacks.

"Uh, let me go change," he said. "Good to see you, Mr. Sunfellow." He left the room and Mom stared after him.

"Yo-Yo! Benjamin!" she cried.

5 Mither

Diary,

Yo-Yo endured getting pinched on the cheeks and Benny squirmed in Mither's tight hugs. Dither just shook hands. He kept quiet mostly. He was hard of hearing and he didn't talk much, but I liked him. His smell seemed reassuring, easygoing, and trustworthy.

Mither and Dither completely changed their clothing just for dinner! Mither still kept her cross on, as bright and shiny as a star.

"Prudence," Mither said, turning to me.

"Yes, Grandmother Sunfellow?" I said stiffly.

Mom had told me to be on my best behavior. I blew at my bangs that hung like comforting cat whiskers.

"Do call me Granny, dear child. Tell me about your school," Mither said.

Dither said squarely, "What's that you said, Mither? Don't bother the child. Let her alone."

I cheered him on in my head.

"Oh, Dither, turn up your hearing aid!" snapped Mither. She cocked her head at me and coaxed me with her eyes.

"I am going to Fairview Middle School next year," I said. I heard Mom and Dad banging pots and pans in the kitchen.

Mither absentmindedly folded a discarded sweater and placed it on top of one of my Mom's brown clay pots.

Yo-Yo and Benny were spending the night at a friend's house, probably so they could skateboard without parents around, and Mom and Dad were in the kitchen. How could they leave me with Mither?

"Dinner!" Dad called, clanging a wooden spoon on the tin bell he got in Japan before he met Mom.

Mither stood up and I took Dither's hand. We slowly went into the dining room.

6 Cholesterol

Diary,

We all sat down at the table. Mom proudly set down a mountain of popping and sizzling fried chicken that made my stomach go berserk, a big homemade crockery bowl full of sugar-butter beans, a platter of steaming baked potatoes with chives, and a heated pot of rich brown French roast coffee.

Dither toyed with the edge of the tablecloth.

Mither spoke up. "Oh, Dana, darling, we never eat fried foods! Too high in cholesterol for Dither's poor heart. Isn't that right, Dither?"

Dither nodded slowly and mournfully.

"Oh, I didn't realize...," Mom trailed off. Her face turned red and her eyes glistened.

I felt sorry for her. I didn't care about cholesterol. I heaped four pieces of fried chicken onto my plate.

"Prudence, toooo much cholesterol!!" Mither

crooned. With her fingers she took three pieces of chicken off my plate. I put them back.

"I eat what I eat!" I said, forgetting my manners.

Mom put her head in her hands for a minute, and I thought she would really start crying.

Dad touched her back, and she pulled her head up.

"Beans?" she asked.

"Do they have butter?" Mither said.

Mom nodded.

"Tsk, tsk, his heart, I'm afraid," she almost sang.

Dither watched me devour a piece of chicken.

Mom sighed. She held up the plate of potatoes.

"We mostly stick to whole grains, dear," Mither said. She patted Dither on the back. "Don't we, Dither?"

He shook his head sadly.

I just wanted to squeeze him in a big walloping hug, but I didn't. I ate some potatoes instead.

"Coffee?" Dad offered, rubbing Mom's slumped back.

"Not if it's caffeinated, Bill," Mither stopped him from pouring. "It stunts your growth."

A tear slid down Mom's cheek, but she smeared it away. "Is there something I can get you...?" Mom said, standing up.

"No need, I came prepared!" Mither said triumphantly. She produced a Tupperware container full of slushy green muck. "Spinach paste," she said, "and mashed lentils!"

7 Religion

Diary,

Today, at breakfast, it was all chaos.

Mither woke up at dawn and began puttering around, cleaning.

Dither went out for a walk.

I tried to sleep, but it was useless once Mither began vacuuming.

I heard Mom get up and Dad jump in the shower.

Finally, I got up, pulled on a yellow t-shirt, sandals, and cutoffs. I went into the kitchen.

Mom was fixing coffee, and Mither was making breakfast. I put my hand on my heart. What was Mither making?

"Oh, good morning, Prudence," she said. She was in a blue dress and her blue cardigan. Her legs were poking out, fat and patterned with crisscrossing blue veins. Her clunky shoes were tied so tightly little rolls of ankle fat spilled over the sides.

"What's for breakfast?" I asked.

"Non-fat fruit granola with yogurt," Mither replied.

"We never have stuff like that," I said.

Mom gave me a little kick.

"What do you usually have, Prudence?" Mither asked, raising an eyebrow. Her gnarled yellow fingernails dug into my arm.

"Uh...eggs...toast," I said.

"Calories! Cholesterol! Granola with yogurt is the trick," Mither said. "Isn't that right, Dana?"

Mom nodded.

The door burst open and the boys came in.

"Yuba! Benjamin!" Mither said. She gave them each a hug and set down bowls full of granola and yogurt on the table.

"We ate breakfast already," the boys said. They escaped into the backyard.

Dad came in and the four of us sat down.

I crunched my granola half heartedly.

Dither came back and began eating too.

"So, Dana, I know you don't like to discuss it, but what about this issue of the children's religion? I know this wonderful priest, Father Brown, who would gladly baptize the children. Catholic, of course," Mither said.

Mom put down her spoon and Dad stopped munching. He's Jewish, and Mom's Catholic. Us kids aren't any religion. Mom and Dad said we could choose when we're ready.

"Mither, drop the subject," Mom said.

"I will not! You were born Catholic! And so were your children," Mither said.

Dither slowly chewed and kept his eyes on his bowl.

"Margaret, please. We are letting the children decide. Now, I think that's enough," Dad said sternly.

Mom looked scared.

"So you are going to let the children ruin their lives? Well, we're not going to just sit here while you do it." Mither stood up and took Dither by the arm. "I think we've overstayed our welcome anyway. Dana, we will expect you and the children at Christmas," she sniffed, and she pulled Dither out of the room.

8 Pudding-Head

Diary,

Did I happen to mention I am only writing this because Mrs. Prince, my fourth grade teacher, wanted my class to do summer diaries? With private thoughts, ideas, creations, and explanations? She is also going to teach my fifth grade class. She says she's always wanted to teach the higher grades and this is her chance to do it and still be with us. And it's her chance to give us homework over the summer! She promised she wouldn't read ours, but I bet she will.

Hey, ol' Prince! Are you reading this? Mrs. Prince, you wanted us to write at least every other day, am I right? Hmmm? You never said we had to use proper grammar and punctuation, did you? Don't be shocked. And please don't read any further.

★ ★ ★

Today, I didn't want to write but I forced myself.

I took one of Mom's crockery pitchers she made with white daisies on it, filled it with freshly sharpened pencils, got my notebook, sat out under the magnolia bush in the backyard, and wrote.

The boys didn't bug me because Mom told them the magnolia bush was my spot. The rest of the yard was theirs.

I already had an orange crate full of books, an old can of V-8, and a sketch pad under the bush. I set to work.

Yesterday afternoon, Mither and Dither left, back to Florida. I could practically hear everything sigh with relief, the refrigerator to the clods of flowers in front of the house. I did sort of miss Dither, though. He seemed so nice and lonely. I wonder, why did he ever marry Mither?

Now I'm all mixed up about religion. I definitely don't want to be Catholic, it would give Mither too much pleasure.

I've met Dad's parents. They were as crazy as he is! They both had bushy gray hair, just like Dad's hair. Except Dad's hair is still brown.

But Mom, I can't believe she is Mither's daughter, because she acts even crazier than Dad.

Okay. Let's get off crazy people. I can't believe

I've written so little and I've been under this bush for two hours, my pencil scratching away, doodlings mixing with the humming of bees swarming in and out of white magnolia blossoms.

★ ★ ★

I took a break to go buy some skim milk for Mom at the 7-11.

Guess who I saw? Ol' Austen Russel, kicking glass around the parking lot.

Suddenly, I started to sweat horribly and my hair hung thick and heavy, weighing me down. My legs felt like Jell-O.

Austen was in a blue striped rugby t-shirt, jeans, and sneakers. His brown hair flopping over his sunburned grinning face.

What was so heart-stopping?

I shook my head and ran into the 7-11. The bell tinkled, before Austen could pause and call, "Pudding-Head! Wait up! What's the rush?"

I was just about to purchase the milk, when Austen snuck up behind me.

"Hi. Whatcha doin', Pudding-Head?" He tossed his head, flicking his long bangs out of his eyes.

"What does it look like I'm doing?" I managed

to croak. I took the milk and my change and walked out.

"Well, see ya 'round, Pudding-Head!" Austen called, racing away.

9 Hormones

Diary,

Dear Mrs. Prince,

This is embarrassing. I beg you not to read further. I'll write in this every day if you just, please, stop reading. Thank you.

Sincerely,

Prudence Mary Frances Brinker

★ ★ ★

All right.

I went to the magnolia bush again with a cold glass of lemonade, a plate of hot cookies I made, my notebook, and a fresh pitcher of pencils.

Mom came by around noon. "Hi, honey. What is my Chickabiddy Baby writing?" she asked.

"Stuff," I replied.

"Well maybe after you write some 'stuff,' you could look at this book I picked up for you. How about it?" Mom said. She placed a book in my lap. It was titled <u>Teenage Hormones</u> by Cathy Sunfellow.

Cathy Sunfellow is my aunt who writes books like my Dad, but lives in a nudist colony. Mom and Dad believe that this is normal. She moved to the nudist colony last year when she divorced Uncle Dan. Actually, he divorced her, because he thought she was eccentric. And she is. She always wears a fluffy pink feather boa, and talks about fallopian tubes and insects.

"Okay, I'll give it a look," I said.

"Good. It's about growing up mostly. Mind if I stay here with you?" She was sitting with her legs crossed in front of the magnolia bush.

"Sure, I guess. Just please don't look at what I am writing," I answered.

"Sure," Mom said. She crawled in and took a sip of lemonade. She held the cool glass to her forehead.

"Ugh. I've got this gigundo headache," she said.

It was so quiet.

"Where are the boys?" I asked.

"I sent them swimming with your Dad. They gave me this headache," Mom said. She closed her eyes and lay down with the lemonade balanced on her head.

I flipped through the <u>Teenage Hormones</u> book. I came to chapter eight: "Changes and Hormones." It said:

> Teenagers and Hormones: Your body will produce hormones that may make you want to go on dates and kiss all the boys you see.
>
> Changing Feelings: You may feel strange, sweaty, or tingly when you see a boy you like. Or you may begin to break out in sobs, or get upset in other ways, more often than before. Don't be scared; it's just your body changing faster than you have expected.

It said more, but I stopped to think about it.

I sorta had those hormones! Sorta about Austen! Why? Why did I sorta like Austen when he called me "Pudding-Head"?

10 The Grays

Diary,

Today somebody moved in across the street. A girl with bob-cut black hair, braces, and big feet, a middle-aged woman with sandy colored hair curled in ringlets, and a boy who was enormously cute!

"Who are they?" I asked Mom as I watched the movers weave between two trees and disappear into the house.

Mom looked up. She was at the kitchen table, gulping iced tea and staring at a mound of brown, lifeless clay.

"Oh, the Grays. I met Ms. Gray at the supermarket. She said she had a daughter and a son and was going to move here in a couple of weeks," she murmured.

Dad came in, staring blankly into a mug of coffee.

"Grays? Who are they? Dana, I can't write, I'm

stuck," he said. He was wet again, fresh out of the tub.

"Well, I can't think of anything to sculpt. The Grays are moving in across the street. Nice woman," Mom said, taking another swig of iced tea.

"Say! I've got it!" Dad cried suddenly. He raced into the bathroom, slammed the door, and began hacking away on his ol' Corona typewriter.

Yo-Yo and Benny trooped into the kitchen.

"I'm bored," Benny whined.

"I'm hungry," Yo-Yo complained.

"Build a fort," Mom said.

"Yeah! Great! Thanks, Mom!" Yo-Yo yelled. He grabbed an apple and they banged back outside.

Mom rubbed her temples. "Ugh! I cannot sculpt today!"

"I've got an idea, Mom," I said.

"What, Chickabiddy Baby?"

"I could bring them some Kool-Aid and cookies," I said.

"Who?" Mom asked, puzzled.

"The Grays."

"I suppose…," Mom mused.

"Great!" I went into the pantry and found some strawberry Kool-Aid mix and a half-eaten package of chocolate chip cookies.

"Mom, can I use the crystal pitcher?" I asked.

"Why? It's such a nice one...well, I guess it would be okay. Go ahead," Mom said. "Need any help?"

"No thanks," I replied. I dumped the cookies on a yellow platter Mom made. I grabbed the pitcher and mixed up the Kool-Aid. Then I ran into the front hall and checked myself twice in the hall mirror.

Brown hair in a ponytail, blue tank top, khaki shorts, and sandals.

What if the boy was cuter than Austen? What if the girl didn't like me? What if one of them was allergic to Kool-Aid? I worried.

"Shut up," I told myself. I grabbed the food and left the house.

Some Kool-Aid sloshed onto my legs. Oh well.

I rang the bell across the street.

" 'Scuse me, girlie," a mover said, carrying a box labeled "junk."

I stepped to one side of the big green wrap-around porch. The door swung open and a woman stepped out.

"Hello," she said.

"Hi, uh, I live across the street. You met my mom? Grocery shopping? Mrs. Brinker?" I said nervously. I felt some Kool-Aid dribble into my sock.

"Oh, yes, of course! Wun-der-ful! Nice to meet you. I'm Susie Gray. Call me Susie. And you are?"

"Prudence Brinker. I brought a little snack. Welcome to the neighborhood," I said.

"Oh my! Thank you! Thank you very much. Let me go get Iris and Jason," Susie said, taking the platter out of my arms. "Take a seat." She dodged a mover and disappeared inside.

I sat on a wicker rocker that was on the porch near four chairs and a small wicker table.

I supposed that Iris and Jason were her kids, that girl and boy I had seen.

Susie reappeared, towing the black-haired girl.

"Sit. Iris, this is Prudence, Prudence, this is my daughter, Iris. Jason can't get away from his new video game, so he'll be down in a little while," she said.

Iris sat on the porch rail and her mom on a chair facing me. Susie placed the snack on the small wicker table.

"So, Prudence, what grade will you be in this fall?" Susie asked.

"Fifth. At Fairview," I said.

"Oh my! Same as Iris! She's going to attend Fairview. She just turned eleven. She started school late," Susie said, a pinched smile on her lips. She had paper cups and napkins. She daintily poured the Kool-Aid and put a cookie on each napkin.

"Wow! You have really long hair! You can sit on it! Whenever my hair gets long, my mom always hacks it off," Iris said.

Susie twisted uncomfortably in her seat and passed me a cup and napkin.

I sipped my Kool-Aid politely.

"I can't wait until July!" Iris crowed.

"Why?" I asked her.

"That's when I get my braces off. Braces are such a nag! I had to get them just because I had a little overbite!" Iris said, staring at her mom, who was slowly shredding her napkin.

Suddenly a boy galloped onto the porch. His hair was a mane of shaggy dirty-blonde curls, shining like straw. His eyes were green and his cheekbones bumped up under perfect freckled cheeks. His face came alive with freckles that also ran down his arms and legs. Boy, was he cuuuuute!

I became self-conscious of my Kool-Aid red legs and began tugging at my hair.

"Hey, Rapunzel!" he said, grinning and shaking back that gorgeous hair.

"Yeah, yeah. This is the family beauty, no braces," Iris said sourly. "This is Jason."

11 A Swimming Invitation

Diary,

"Well, how old is he!? What's he like!?" Mouse screamed. It sounded like she was right next to me, instead of in South Dakota. I held the phone away from my ear. I was telling her about Jason.

"Weeeeeeelllll!!!!" Mouse screeched, stretching out the short word as long as it could go.

"Well, he's thirteen. Really cute. A nice sense of humor. He called me Rapunzel. And that's about it," I said. Why should I tell her the facts, if I liked him? I was jealous. But of who?

Mouse told me her cousin's friend had a best friend and the best friend had taken her swimming.

The doorbell rang.

"Mouse, I've gotta go," I said.

"Okay, I'll call later. Bye," Mouse said. The phone clicked.

I ran into the front hall.

It was Iris. She was in a tight yellow bathing suit with bows all over it and a big bow in back. It was ridiculous.

"Hi Iris," I said. "Come on in."

She stepped inside. She was holding a purple towel. Her face was red.

"I hate this suit," she said. "My mom got it for me."

"Oh. Want something to drink? Cola? Lemonade?" I said.

"Well, actually, no thanks, I just came to ask if you wanted to go swimming with me and Jason. I'm practicing my swan dive. My mom wants me to be in competitive swimming. But if she wants me to wear this suit, she can forget it!" Iris said. The last sentence came out as a snarl. It really seemed like she hated her mom.

"I have to baby-sit my brothers...," I trailed off. Jason would be there! "Hang on a minute. Have a drink." I found Mom sculpting.

"Do you mind if I'm gone for a couple of hours? Swimming with the Grays? I baby-sat five hours last Tuesday," I begged.

"The Grays? Oh, how nice! Is Iris sweet?" Mom asked. She was making a big brown pot to add to the collection of our other pots in the dining room.

"Yes, yes. Can I?" I asked.

"Sure. But be back by four. I need you to watch the boys while I go to a party with your father. I'll give you five dollars. Deal?" Mom finished.

"Deal."

I ran into my room and tore around, looking for my bathing suit. I finally found it. It's purple with a diagonal magenta stripe. It shows a lot of my back. I pulled it on. I have big bumps on my chest now. (Mrs. Prince! Quit reading!) Bigger than last year. They made my bathing suit tighter than it had been. I put on my sandals, pulled my hair into a braid, and grabbed a beach towel. I went back out on the front porch where Iris was, sipping a soda.

"You can come!? Great! I'm so glad I've got a friend!"

12 Up in the Clouds

Diary,

La deeee dah!

Yesterday was grrreat!

I can't write. I'll write tomorrow. My brain is toooo mushy. I think Jason liiiikes meeeee!

13 Poetry

Diary,

Today, I got my summer reading list like I get every single year from school. They were late this year, so Mrs. Prince had to mail it. The list said:

The Sword in the Stone
T. H. White
Little Women
Louisa May Alcott
Roll of Thunder, Hear My Cry
Mildred D. Taylor
Sadako and the Thousand Paper Cranes
Eleanor Coerr
Blue Willow
Doris Gates
Running Out of Time
Margaret Peterson Haddix

> Please choose 2 to 6 books.
> Read them, and write down your reactions to
> the books.

So I went to the library and got <u>Little Women</u>, which was about a billion pages long, and <u>Roll of Thunder, Hear My Cry</u>. I started <u>Roll of Thunder, Hear My Cry</u>. I read chapter one and recorded my notes.

<u>Roll of Thunder</u>
Chapter 1: I think it's unfair how little black
kids have to go to schools that aren't
equipped as well as where the white kids go.
My favorite part was when Cassie says, "I
don't want my book neither." She was brave to
stand up for herself.

I decided to write some poetry. I was so bored with taking notes. I've never written poetry before. If it's bad I can tear it out.

<u>Fall</u>
Howling in like a lion,
leaves swirling in an angry dance,

dancing across the hills,
right into my open window,
blowing my candle out.

Now, here's what happened last night:

The boys and I stayed up playing crazy eights and watching <u>The Mummy's Tomb</u>, which gave me nightmares and the absolute willies! It was ten-thirty, past the boys' bedtime, but they begged to stay up. The clock bonged eleven. Bong, bong, bong, bong, bong, bong, bong, bong, bong, bong, bong.

"C'mon, it's time for bed!" I said.

"I'm scared," Benny said, chewing his finger-nails.

Yo-Yo clonked him on the head. "Scaredy-cat!" he hissed. But he was as white as a sheet.

Moonlight flooded the room and cool air wafted in from the open window. Benny banged it shut.

"I'll take you up," I said, trying to be brave.

Benny made sure I locked everything. Then I turned on all the lights and the stereo, pretty loud. Finally, the boys went to bed. As soon as I shut the door, their bedroom light clicked on. I let them leave it on. I went in the kitchen and closed all the curtains. My skin felt like it was curdling. The whole house creaked. I shivered and turned on the TV. I found a rerun of <u>Gilligan's Island</u>. I left it on while I puttered around the house, picking things up, dusting brown pots, closing drapes, skimming books. I finally turned off the TV, but left everything else on, and got into bed, only pulling off my shoes. I pulled the sheet up to my chin and rolled over, facing the wall.

I went to sleep. I guess I slept for half an hour. A mummy was chasing me around a maze and I fell in a black hole. Then I woke up, sweating cold sweat.

My room was covered in silky, silvery moonlight. It washed over the rug, and my glow-in-the-dark stars were glowing like menacing eyes.

I squeezed my eyes shut tight. But they flew open when I heard footsteps on the stairs and a strange thin voice singing, "Good-bye, so lonnng... I'm in the mood for loooove!"

My door swung open.

A shadowy figure with two arms and four legs was slumped in the doorway!

It was Dad, holding Mom around the waist.

She was holding her pearls and a high-heeled shoe. She was wearing a black cocktail dress and a fake Indian headdress.

"Loooove! Looove! Bill...let go!" she whispered

loud. She flailed her arms, whacking her shoe against the wall. Her string of pearls broke.

"Shhhhh...," Dad pleaded.

"Dad, what's wrong?" I asked, crouching closer to the wall.

"Go to sleep, honey. Your mother had a little too much to drink," Dad said. He towed Mom away, slowly letting the door click shut.

14 A Hangover

Diary,

In the morning, Mom stayed in bed. I found her pearls crushed. She had an enormous headache and only ate Advil. She said she felt like a bunch of wildebeest were stampeding in her head. She skipped breakfast and lunch.

"What's the matter with Mom?" Benny asked.

"She has a hangover. Shhhh," Dad said. Benny nodded, like he knew what a hangover was. Mostly we just tiptoed around the house all day. I read chapter two of <u>Roll of Thunder, Hear My Cry</u> while I was fixing frozen meatloaf for supper.

Mouse called twice and then Iris said she was planning a party once her family was all settled in and she would be sure to invite me. I went to my favorite ice cream shop, FlavorBest. I saw Austen. I can't decide who I like more between him and Jason. For one thing, Jason is older.

I'm too lazy to write. Besides, my pencil scratching might wake Mom. Geez! Is she acting crotchety!

15 Mouse

Diary,

Mouse came home today! She burst out of her parents' car and I watched her run to our front door from my window.

I was upstairs in my room with Iris.

And oh Deity! Marjorie looked really different! Her red, frizzy hair was permed and crimped. And she was skinny. She used to be fat, no offense. She was twirling a pennant and her face was clogged up with purple eye shadow.

"Who's that?" Iris asked, throwing her big feet over the side of the bed and flopping over to the window.

"Marjorie, Mouse, an old friend," I said.

"Oh. I seeeee. Hmmmm. Do you like her?" Iris said slowly.

I shrugged. "Sorta. I've known her since pre-school. It's kind of hard to ignore her, if you know what I mean."

"Ohhhh. I seeeeee. Should I goooooo?" Iris slowly said. That long, slow talking was kind of getting on my nerves. Was it so wrong that I had another friend?

"Nope, stay. I'd like to introduce you to her," I said.

"Is she niiiiiiiiiiiccce? Prrruuuudence? Will I like her? You know, I can goooo hoooome, if you waaaaant. If I'll be in the waaaaayyy. Huuuuuuuh?" Iris stretched the words out just like Mouse did over the telephone.

"Iris! Stay!" I shouted.

I heard Mouse pounding up the stairs. She flung open the door.

"Pru—," she stopped. "Who's that!?" She pointed a quaking finger at Iris, who was wearing a big blue sweater and a pink skirt which showed her long legs.

"Mouse, this is my new friend, Iris. Iris, this is my friend, Mouse," I said. I quickly added, "Shake hands."

They did, slowly, looking each other over, up and down.

"Nice meeting you. Pru, please don't call me Mouse anymore. I have to run. Toodle-oo!" Mouse pounded back down the stairs and burst outside.

Iris and I talked about school under the magnolia bush, then she went home.

Mom was napping, but she felt a little better.

Dad insisted that we still had to tiptoe.

God, excuse me, Deity, footsteps sound like firecrackers to her! I'm glad nobody knows she has a hangover. That would be sooo embarrassing!

16 The Jealousy of Jason

Diary,

Today Iris invited Marjorie and me to go swimming with her and Jason. I was so afraid that Jason would like Mouse, I mean Marjorie, more.

When Marjorie and I were changing she said, "Jason is just gor-gee-ous! Just wait until he sees me in my new bathing suit! I got it in South Dakota."

But Mouse had an ugly olive-green and puke-yellow bathing suit. She strutted around in it, acting like she was really something. She doesn't even have bumps on her chest yet. Iris does, but they are hidden by the bows on her suit.

"But I thought you said you liked that other boy," I said, coiling my braided hair around my head and stabbing the braid with bobbypins.

"Oh, Devon? Well yeah, I guess, but he's all the way in South Dakota!" Marjorie said.

"How's your summer diary going? I'm really getting into mine. I already filled up my notebook. I need another," I said, changing the subject.

"Augh! I hate my diary! It's only about eight pages long," Marjorie replied. She modeled her ugly suit and struck a pose. "Weeeeellll?" she demanded.

I noticed all the bug bites on her legs and sunburned, peeling skin on her back. How could Jason like her more?

We walked to the pool and Mouse wiggled up to Jason when he climbed out of the pool after cannonballing. Literally, Mouse wiggled!

"Hiiiii, Jaaaassssoooon! Watcha doooooooiiiin'?" she sighed. She batted her eyelids.

"What did you say your name was again?" Jason asked, scratching his thick, wet curls.

Lice, lice, lice! A voice screamed in my head. I've had lice, and it is just horrible! I pinched my arm and my brain shut up.

"Oooohhhh, I'm just Marjorie. You know? Pru's best friend," Marjorie said.

"Unh," Jason just grunted.

Marjorie wiggled her fingers and wiggled over to her towel.

"She's hooked. Definitely hooked. The jealousy of Jason. For my ol' brother!" Iris whispered.

I batted my eyelashes and wiggled my shoulder. I patted my hair. "Ooohhh! Jaaasssooon!" I mocked.

We burst out laughing.

I wasn't so sure yet about telling Iris I liked Jason.

17 The Time Quilt Begins

Diary,

I read chapters three and four today.

Mom is all better. I know she is because she is singing and sculpting again. She called Aunt Cathy on the telephone and they chatted for a total of three and a half HOURS!

She's working on a pot, a huge one, so she just heated up some leftover macaroni and cheese for supper.

And now Mom is also making a quilt. A "time quilt" is what she calls it. She's taking all of our old clothes, including some material and clothing from other places, friends, and the rest of the family, and making all of it into a big quilt of the past. She's hoping that Mouse's mom and Susie Gray will pitch in with some materials and help make the quilt.

Roll of Thunder

Chapter 3: I think it is totally unfair that their school doesn't have buses and how the kids get covered with dirt on the way to school.

Also, Jeremy seems really nice.

WOW! They really ditch that bus! And serves 'em right!

Chapter 4: I'm too lazy to write notes. I'm just glad I don't have to churn butter like Cassie does!

Later...

Chapter 4: That was one heck of a fight! Wowee! Yo-Yo got a shiner once, but that's because he ran into a table.

Susie Gray and Mary Ellis, Marjorie's mom, came over with bundles of old materials and clothing, all the way back from their great grandmothers! They cleared away a big spot in the living room, stuffing stray clothing and magazines into scattered big brown pots. Then they started cutting out squares.

Mom put me in charge of recording the daily work on the quilt. Then I jotted down:

THE TIME QUILT
Day 1: Cut out quilt squares.

Iris invited me and Marjorie over to her house. We played CDs up in her room.

Jason popped in. "Rapunzel! Frizzy! Long-time-no-see!" he said. He calls Mouse "Frizzy," but she acts like he is calling her "Beautiful." Mouse told me he just calls her Frizzy because he likes her.

Rapunzel sounds more, uh, well, nice. I shut my mouth, though. What if Iris made fun of me?

Marjorie smiled and batted her purple lids.

Jason sat cross-legged on the bed next to me. "Sis, you still haven't finished unpacking?" he said to Iris, flicking back his hair.

I tingled. Then I looked out the window and saw Austen Russel riding his bike! Ugh! How am I going to be able to choose who I like between Austen and Jason?

18 A Bunch o' Malarkey

Diary,

Today I really forced myself to write. I took the <u>Teenage Hormones</u> book, <u>Roll Of Thunder, Hear My Cry</u>, this notebook (my second), a can of V-8, and a plate of cookies, all out to the magnolia bush.

Dad was playing catch with the boys. The moms were working on the quilt. I had already recorded:

Day 2: Still gathering and cutting squares.

Okay, I'm getting way off the point here. Let me start. Yesterday afternoon Marjorie called me. Let's pretend it was a movie. It goes like this:

KITCHEN SCENE BRIGHTENS
Prudence Brinker is making cookies. A sweet aroma wafts around the kitchen.

The telephone rings.

Prudence drops her spatula and picks up the telephone receiver.

ME: Hello?

MOUSE: Hi! This is Marjorie. Guess whaaaaat?

ME: (Stretched out words are getting on my nerves.) Whaaaaaaat?

MOUSE: Weeeelllllll. Hmmmmmm. Now where should I begiiiiiin?

ME: I don't know, you haven't told me yet. I think you should start at the beginning.

MOUSE: Oookaaaayyy. Let me gather it uuup. (Taking her time.)

ME: C'mon! I have cookies baking!

MOUSE: All right, all right alreeeaaaady!! Weeeelllll...Austen took me out to ice cream! At the FlavorBest! We held hands, and talked, just like boyfriend and girlfriend.

ME: (A wave of anger washes over me.) What about Jason? (Geez! Mouse was acting like she was getting married!)

MOUSE: What about Jason?

ME: Oh, this is a bunch of malarkey, I'm telling you!

MOUSE: Well Gawd, you don't have to get all mad at meeee!

ME: Deity, Marjorie! Have Austen, you pimple-head! You *are* malarkey!

PRUDENCE BANGS DOWN THE TELEPHONE. SCENE FADES OUT

See? These hormones are really catching up to me!

Then there was Iris. She asked me what I wrote in this notebook and why I spent so much time under some old magnolia bush.

I told her I couldn't say, and now she isn't talking to me.

Get the picture? I think everybody is getting these freaked-out hormones!

Oh! And then there's Jason. But it's too great to tell and my brain turns to porridge when I hear his name, so I'll write all about it tomorrow.

Yawn. Good night.

19 Dream Candles

Diary,

Before I tell you about Jason, wonderful Jason, I want to tell you about Iris. We're friends again, but she is making waaaay tooo many puns! (Now I am sounding like Mouse.) Puns, puns, puns aaalllll (Mouse again) day! (I'm exaggerating.)

I spent the day with her and with (sigh, sigh) Jason.

I was making breakfast for myself (eggs sprinkled with garlic and cheese), when Iris called.

It was almost ten o'clock and Mom and Dad were at the early movies with the boys. I've already seen the movie twice. And of course it is PG. I'm only allowed to see PG movies. Isn't that bizarre?

Well, back to this morning. The telephone rang, and I picked it up while I stirred my eggs. "Hello?"

"Hi, it's me, Iris. Did you eat any breakfast yet?" Iris said.

"Nope," I replied.

"Are you making it?" she asked.

"Yup."

"What?"

"Eggs."

"Hey, that's eggs-actly what I had!" Iris screeched. I could just imagine her rocking with laughter.

"Huh. Nice pun," I muttered.

"Hey, thanks! Hey, I have one more! How do you hide a camel caravan from another caravan?" Iris cried.

"I have absolutely no clue," I grumbled.

"Give up?" she sang, plainly tickled.

"Uh, yeah, I have utterly no idea."

"With camel-flage!" Iris shrieked triumphantly.

"Oooohhhh...uh, really funny," I said.

"I know! I have one more!"

"Iris...," I whined.

"Oh, puh-lease? You'll love this one!" Iris whined back.

"Oh, all right. But hurry up, my eggs will burn," I muttered.

"Oh, goody! What does a dog say before he eats something really good?"

I had heard this one before, but I didn't want to spoil Iris's fun.

"I have no idea."

"He says bone-appetite!" Iris totally cracked up.

"Haha...." I tapped my foot. "Iris, why exactly did you call me?"

"Oh, I was wondering if you wanted to come over and make dream candles with me and Jason? He learned how to make them in some class," Iris said.

"Sure! I'll be right over as soon as I finish breakfast! Bye!" I hung up. Jason! I twirled around the kitchen.

After breakfast I climbed up the stairs two at a time. I took twenty minutes choosing an outfit. Do I sound crazy? I finally chose a pair of my favorite leather sandals with the gold butterfly buckles, a pair of sky-blue shorts, a sky-blue shirt, and a blue sweater with little brown-and-white kittens all over it. I braided my hair in a thick, long braid, just like Rapunzel, and lathered my legs up with Mom's lilac-rose lotion.

I ran over to Iris's and rang the bell. It rang, loudly, echoing in the house.

Footsteps pounded on the stairs inside. The door burst open and there stood Jason, as cute as ever! He was in a BAD DOG t-shirt, ripped up jeans, and clunky hiking boots. Not exactly the god of creation, but you know, the styles these days.

"Hey, Rapunzel. Where's Frizzy?" he said. He shook my hand, and my stomach turned into a bunch of electric sparks.

I smiled. I think I looked dumb. Lame-brain! a voice screamed in my head. So I finally blurted, "Hi. Mouse, er, Marjorie couldn't make it."

"Ah, I see. But you could make it. Great, now Iris will quit telling puns to me, and start telling you," Jason said. He laughed. Then he let go of my hand and my stomach settled down, a bit. He led me into their big, old, colonial-style kitchen.

The table was covered with newspapers.

Iris was at the table, munching on crackers. "Hi! I'm so glad you came!" she squealed.

Jason nudged me and an electrifying spark shot through me again. "Wait for the puns," he said through gritted teeth.

I had to hold my breath to keep from laughing. (Sigh.)

I couldn't take my eyes off Jason. Well, I'm exaggerating. I could, but he was so close, right next to me, his hands opening old milk cartons, sometimes brushing my hands. (This may sound like a bunch of mush, but it is the story.)

The candles were to be made in milk cartons and when they came out they were to have Swiss-cheese-looking holes and curves, funnels, and passages for the dreams to come through.

I can't remember exactly how we made them. All I remember is Jason said he liked mine.

We dropped in crayons so they would be colored when they were all done. I put orchid and silver, dreamy sort of colors.

I am going to put mine by my bed when it's done.

I can't wait to dream about things—especially about Jason.

20 Trouble and $18.50

Diary,

Aaaargh! Oh no! Blech! Blah! Hmmm. What news should I tell about first? I guess about the library book, <u>Roll of Thunder, Hear My Cry</u>. All right, calm down, Prudence. Here goes....

Today the moms gathered to work on the quilt again.

I recorded what they did and then looked for <u>Roll of Thunder</u>. I figured it was under my bed or some other place simple like that. I looked everywhere, no exaggerating! I asked Mom if she would help me look, but she said she had to work on that dumb quilt.

Mom looked sooo embarrassing! She was wearing torn up sweatpants, a paint-spattered t-shirt, and Dad's old, ratty tennis shoes. And she kept laughing loudly, sounding exactly like a horse.

And Dad was being really embarrassing too,

flopping around the house in his wet clothes, his wild, frizzed-out hair tangled around his head.

"Einstein, oh Mad Professor!" Mom called to him.

"Yes, Sugar Pie?" Dad asked.

"Change your clothes, or you'll catch pneumonia!" Mom called back.

Mary Ellis and Susie exchanged glances.

I stomped away, exasperated.

"Benny, have you seen my book, the big, fat one? The one with the African-American girl on the front?" I asked Benny, who was playing matchbox cars with Yo-Yo.

Benny ran a red sports car up my sleeve. "Uh-huh."

"Where!?" I shouted, grabbing him by both his shoulders.

"W-w-weeeeellllllllllllll...," he stuttered. He sounded exactly like Mouse.

"I took it outside. Oh! Don't be mad at me! I just wanted to read it—or try—then by accident it went in the sprinklers, and then, well, I dropped it in the bushes, then I dropped it in the mud and then, well...it fell apart," Benny finished.

"Oh Deity! Holy Moses! Geez Louise! Man, oh man!" I flopped down onto the grass.

Yo-Yo stared at me, then at Benny. "He put it in the garbage, I saw!" he said with triumph.

I whistled. "Well, you have to tell Mom, not me! March!" I told Benny.

He slowly went inside, giving me dirty looks as if this was all my fault.

Yo-Yo turned to me. "Whatsit gonna cost?" he asked.

"A lot," I muttered. I went inside.

Benny was telling the whole story while Mom's face slowly turned from peach to yellow to white.

★ ★ ★

We went to the library.

While I tried to settle down Yo-Yo and Benny, Mom whispered with the librarian.

I heard the librarian say, "Hardcover books usually cost from eighteen dollars and fifty cents to twenty dollars."

Mom smacked her forehead with her hand and opened her purse. She fumbled, then pulled out two wrinkled ten-dollar bills and handed them to the librarian. I could tell she was cooking mad.

I bet if Mither was there she would give Benny a good spanking.

21 Austen

Diary,

I saw Mouse and Austen at FlavorBest. Austen looked as bored as anything, Mouse yakking her head off, talking about, of all things, cosmetics. Like he cares!

I was with Iris. When Mouse saw us come in, she started making eyes at Austen. He was red, aside from his sunburn. Iris nudged me.

"Who's that with Marjorie?" she asked. I glanced, acting as if I couldn't care less.

"Why, that's Austen Russel. He's from Martin School, too. He moved here from Riverdale last year," I said.

Iris stared into her strawberry-raspberry icee. I turned again to watch Austen. Marjorie was discussing Revlon. Austen was fiddling with his straw. He looked up, saw me looking. He grinned and mouthed "Pudding-Head." I smiled and, embarrassed, turned back to my ice cream sundae.

Dad was complaining about how his book on Vietnam was in the dumps. Mom suggested he write some poetry. Mary Ellis and Susie and Mom went on a hike and on a picnic, to work on the quilt away from Dad. Dad wrote poetry all day, shut up in his study. When Mom got home, he said he was in a writer's rut. That's his way of saying "I'm stuck, I still can't write." So then Mom suggested we spend a couple weeks up at the lake, and rent a summer house like we did last year. Dad said it was a wonderful idea. While he made bread and Mom potted, they discussed the possibilities. They decided to celebrate the fourth of July here, though.

Uck! I don't want to go to Lake Pinegrove! Last time we went, it was so boooooooooooooooring!!!!

Mom was so embarrassing. She tasted the bread and began talking with her mouth full. Parents!

Yawn. I'm sleepy.

22 The First Note

Diary,

Iris is really excited. Her braces are coming off in four days, and I'm going to the lake in four days. I do not want to go! Benny and Yo-Yo are as excited as Mom and Dad. Luckily we are renting a different house. The last one we rented had a big hole in the wall that we covered with a sheet, but still, raccoons gnawed their way in. Freaky! One morning, Mom woke up and found one curled up at the foot of her bed! (And I am not kidding!)

I started <u>Little Women</u>. It's pretty good. I read <u>Eight Cousins</u> which is also by Louisa May Alcott, and it was pretty good. <u>Little Women</u> is exactly 627 pages long. Marjorie faked reading it for the end-of-the-school-year book report. She got a C–.

Well, well, Mrs. Prince, I sure wrote a lot, didn't I? I'm on my third blue notebook. Now here is a bit of interesting news! Today I went out to the magnolia bush. Guess what I found!? A note! Not a love note or something like that. It said:

> When the heart overflows, it comes out
> through the mouth. —Ethiopian proverb

Weird, huh? It made me giddy. It was sort of a love note. It just had to be from Jason! Had to. I showed it to Mom. Bad idea. She bumped me with her rear end and batted her stubby eyelashes.

"Ooooooo," she crooned, "looks like you've got an admirer."

"Mo-om!" I shouted. I grabbed the note and sulked under the magnolia bush. But who knew about my secret place? Why would somebody leave me an Ethiopian proverb?

23 Fourth of July

Fourth of July was a mess. Mom and Dad got in a huge argument, the Grays went to San Francisco, and Mouse was crabby.

24 The Big Idea

Diary,

Today, we packed up to spend two horrible weeks at the lake! I packed one skirt, two pairs of leggings, eight shorts, two pairs of jeans, four blouses, two turtlenecks, three t-shirts, a nightie, and a sweater. Then I threw in a bunch of comics, bubble gum, <u>Little Women</u>, a blank notebook, a dried magnolia blossom, the note, a toothbrush, and twenty pairs of socks and some underwear. I also packed hiking boots and sandals. Missing anything? Yup. I added my bathing suit. I went outside to water my magnolia bush and cover my books beneath it to shield them from the rain. And you can guess what happened. Yup. I found another note. It said:

One who runs alone cannot be outrun by another. —Ethiopian proverb

I showed Dad and something clicked inside of him.

"That's it!" he cried happily, kissing me, then the note, then his old typewriter. I swear, he was acting just like Aunt Cathy, kissing everything.

"What!? What!? What is it!?" I yelled. I hate being kept in suspense.

"I'll write a book of proverbs! Ethiopian...all sorts! This is great! I feel as light as a feather. No more writer's rut! Lake Pinegrove, here we come!" he cried.

Mom came in and Dad scooped up both of us into a hug. He twirled us around. Honestly! Deity. Then he scooped up Benny and Yo-Yo and they screamed with laughter. We piled in the car and were off.

25 Singin' in the Rain

Diary,

Dad excitedly bounced around the curve and pulled up to the little pink real estate agency building to get the keys for our cottage. The lake was right in front of us. The sky was gray, and even though it was hot, it looked like it was going to rain.

All of a sudden, fat raindrops swooshed down in torrents, drowning out the sound of the motor.

"Tut, tut, looks like rain," Mom said. Embarrassing!!!! Benny shrieked and busted open the car door. He scrambled out and started dancing in the rain. Yo-Yo followed him.

"Boys—," Mom called. But she stopped and laughed. She unbuckled her seatbelt and left the car too! And then, Deity, she started dancing! Of all things! Splashing in puddles and singing with the boys. I stuck my head out the window.

"You guys are crazy!" I yelled. Then I slammed

the car door shut and sulked. The real estate people were looking out their windows. How embarrassing! I squeezed out my wet braids. My blue ribbons were splattered with rain. After a couple minutes of watching Mom and the boys, I read some of <u>Little Women</u>—only a paragraph, because then Dad hopped in the car. The boys climbed in, wet and breathless. They climbed over me, soaking me, chilling my skin.

"Get off, jerks!" I said. I was crabby for some reason.

"Getting your period, Prudence?" Mom said, climbing in.

"No! Quit embarrassing me! Deity! You really are crazy!" I yelled. Then I folded my arms and shoved Yo-Yo off me with my foot.

"Mommy," Benny said, "what's a period? Is it that dot on the end of sentences? How come Prudence gets a period, and I don't?"

I burst out laughing. It was going to be a hectic ride.

26 The Lake

Diary,

Dad turned left onto a dirt road. Red dust clouded up under gray raindrops. The rain had lessened to a slight drizzle.

Dad squeezed Mom's left hand as we bounced over rocks and pebbles. A small stream bubbled beside the road.

Finally we pulled into a driveway behind a battered gray cottage with ugly green shutters and big spots of filth and rust. Blech! A rickety wraparound porch was slapped up against the gray frame of the cottage. Pitiful, just pitiful.

Mom stared at it. "Well" was all she could manage to say. She opened the car door and got out. She opened the trunk and started hauling bags up the front steps. Soon we were all lugging luggage onto the porch.

Rain plastered my hair to my head. I gasped in the musty air.

Ten yards from the front of the house lay the lake, slushy, murky, and a brownish green color with green froth on the edges. Algae crept like a thick carpet over the misty surface. A canoe sullenly floated at the side, tied to a tree stump, the rope overgrown with muck.

Mom muttered "Well" again and Dad unlocked the green front door.

Inside it was dark, with only naked bulbs dangling from the ceiling for light. The kitchen had greasy green walls, a rickety card table, a monstrous black stove, and a big ugly refrigerator.

My room, which used to be the storage room, had a high iron bedstead with a lumpy mattress, an old toy chest and dresser, accompanied by cobwebs, a desk that looked like it was from the 1920s, and one solitary window.

The planks that served as floorboards creaked uneasily under my light weight and I noticed wide spaces between each wooden plank.

I slowly unpacked, glancing at the peeling linoleum walls that bubbled from age.

A summer cottage? More like a prison. And guess what—no telephone and no bathroom!

I can't believe it! All we get is an outhouse!! A small chicken coop–sized outhouse! Wooden walls with knotholes, and a putrid odor, like a skunk sprayed in there! But at least it has a small metal toilet. (Even though you can't flush it.)

27 Mackenzie

Diary,

This morning I was walking around the lake in bare feet. Goose bumps were creeping up my legs and arms. It was a very gray morning and very cold. I plopped down on the wet sand and rubbed my legs vigorously. My hair got all sandy at the tips.

I was dying to call Iris or write a letter to her, but the post office was nearly five miles away. And of course there was no telephone except for the pay phone all the way back on the main road.

I edged my toes into the lake and scowled. When I pulled them out of the icy water, they were lined with a thin film of green algae. (Mouse definitely would have cringed.)

"Hello?" someone called from behind me.

I jumped, startled. Flecks of gross water spattered on my yellow t-shirt. I scooped up my sandals and turned.

A tall, tan girl with big white-blonde hair stood several paces away. She was wearing a bright fuschia cardigan, black jeans, a snazzy gold blouse, and hikers. She stood in a pose, and her blue eyes looked me over. She looked like the happy-go-lucky type.

My hair fell over my shoulder and rippled down my back. I straightened up, brushing dirt off my legs. I picked sand out of my hair.

"Hey," the girl said. "I'm Mackenzie."

Who was she? And why was she all dressed up in a dump like this? I guess she must've read my thoughts or something because then she said, "I'm Mackenzie Michelle de Gabriella. I'm visiting from Venice Beach, California. My dad makes soap operas. You see, my dad is also making a line of mansions around the lake, and then he is going to connect them and make them all into a huge, grand resort. Right now we are staying in a motel a couple miles from town. Who are you?"

Deity! She must've stopped because she was out of breath! And she sure was putting on airs. I wonder what she would do if she got love notes like I'd been getting. She would probably broadcast it all over the evening news!

Her white-blonde hair stood out in the thick morning fog like a torch.

"Uh, me? I'm...," I totally blanked out. Should I tell her my name? Would she make fun of it? "I'm Daphne Cappuccino," I blurted. Stupid, stupid, stupid! "I'm staying here with my family. Uh, my dad is a famous author," I flinched. Dad wasn't really famous, but he did get nominated for a Newbery award for his book, Cloud Pancakes.

"Neato! Cool. I love your last name! It is so much better than de Gabriella. Wow! Your dad writes? Bodacious!" Mackenzie's voice dripped like syrup out of her raspberry-lipstick lips. But a sticky tinge of falseness was there, like she was forcing the words out of her mouth. She sounded about half sincere.

I nodded vigorously, slapping a mosquito off my arm. But I reddened with shame from my white lie. Daphne Cappuccino? Why not Daphne Calla Tortilla? Or Daphne Pudding-Head? And why Daphne? I gave myself a little kick. My brain talked too much.

"Well, Daph, it was great meeting you! See you later?" Mackenzie said.

I nodded and grinned, flicking back my hair. It whipped around and hit my cheek so it stung.

"Love the hair!" Mackenzie ran off and I heaved a sigh of relief.

28 Sea Monster

Diary,

The fog burned off around noon today and the sun glared through the gray clouds, giving the lake a glistening, almost eerie, sheen. Mom sewed quilt squares outside while Dad made fresh bread and scribbled notes on a pad of paper. How could he make anything in that place? Benny and Yo-Yo were playing "sea monster" in the lake, in the shallow part. Uck!

I was in my bathing suit, sitting by Mom, sunning myself, and holding <u>Little Women</u>. I didn't feel like reading.

It was warmer, almost hot.

Dad popped his head out the door, scanned the weather, and exclaimed, "Good day to go to the library!" Then he disappeared inside the house.

Slowly the smell of baking bread wafted outside and greeted our noses. Mom poked herself with the needle, cursed, and muttered about getting a new thimble. Her lashes quivered as she creased her forehead which made her lids bunch up. I then thought of how Mary Ellis's lids had been thick musty mauve purple, just like Mouse. This made me giggle, or as Dad liked to say, chortle. What a word.

Mom went for a walk earlier and said she found a shower house. When I said, "So," she said, "Well that's good, then we can rinse off after a swim in the lake. Then we won't have to stay green until we get home."

I agreed with her, but I am not going swimming, N-O-T. Not! I closed my eyes and listened to the boys play.

29 Mrs. Cappuccino

Diary,

<u>Little Women</u>
Chapter 1: I can't imagine Christmas without presents! It just wouldn't be Christmas!

Quilt Records
Day ?: Still cutting squares, but beginning to sew them together.

It is soooo boring here!

At breakfast I watched Benny eat his Cheerios in his special routine. He lets the Cheerios soak up all the milk until they are all soggy, then he mashes them with his teeth into mush, then he swishes it around in his mouth, and then he eats it. Blech!

Yo-Yo eats his Cheerios weirdly, too. He smashes

them up to powder, and then he pours milk on them.

Mom was wolfing down Dad's delicious bread, and Dad was up in his room, typing on his old typewriter. Sometimes I can't believe I was born into this family.

I was done with breakfast, so I finally gathered up my courage to take a swim in the lake. I pulled on my bathing suit, brushed out my hair until it was staticky, and then stuffed it under a bathing cap. I ran and plunged into the icy lake. It was dark and cold. My feet tripped over pebbles and weeds at the bottom. I stood up. Half of my body was in the water, half of it was out. I guess I'm getting taller. I felt my way along the bottom of the lake. About twenty paces from the shore there was a huge drop-off.

I swam, reeds pressing against my skin, swishing back and forth, twisting around me. I swam free-style. It was kind of scary. Then I got out of the water and walked over to the showerhouse, picking twigs off my suit along the way.

I yanked off my suit and cap and rinsed off and then rinsed out my suit. I put it back on and walked back to the cottage.

As I was pulling shorts and a polo on, I heard a

voice call through the screen door, "Heeeyyyy! Hello!?" It was Mackenzie.

I heard the boys answer the door and Mom ask, "Who is it?"

I walked out of my room, combing out my hair. The wooden floorboards dug into my bare feet. I slipped into my butterfly buckle sandals.

"Hi! It's me, Mack. Want to go for a canoe?" Mackenzie called through the screen. She stepped inside. She was wearing tight designer jeans, a magenta sweater, and a black blouse. Snazzy. She was also wearing high-heeled boots and dangly silver earrings. "Hello, Mrs. Cappuccino. I'm Mackenzie de Gabriella. I met your daughter a few days ago," Mackenzie said.

I almost died. Mom smiled absentmindedly. "Oh, how nice. Chickabiddy Baby, sweetie, do you want to go canoeing?"

Thank Deity she didn't realize that Mackenzie had called her Mrs. Cappuccino.

Mackenzie's voice had a sweeter ring to it than before. "Your daughter is safe with me, ma'am. I know all about canoeing." But her voice stumbled over the word "canoeing."

"Well?" Mom said, looking at me.

I shrugged. "Sure, why not, swell."

Mackenzie backed out of the house. "C'mon, let's go," she said.

I tripped over the steps after her.

★ ★ ★

OH NO! Oops. I need another notebook to finish this story! I just filled this one all up. Be back in a jiffy! Aaahh! I'm outta room!!!!

30 White Lies

Diary,

"So, where's the canoe?" I asked.

"There, lame-brain. It's your canoe," Mackenzie said.

I knew how to canoe, I've been doing it at the lake for years, but Mackenzie seemed unsure of herself as she untied the thick rope from the old stump. Her fingers trembled. The white sun burned onto our backs through a thin sheet of cloud. I wondered what a sun-baked cloud pancake would taste like.

"So, what books has your dad written?" Mackenzie asked. She gestured for me to undo the tight knot. Sweat beaded her lip. What a scaredy-cat. My mind raced back and forth.

"Lots, I can't name them all," I blinked uncomfortably. Mackenzie nodded. I flipped off my sandals and waded into the water. Mackenzie looked at the grimy lake in absolute disgust.

"C'mon. Don't you know how to shove off?" I grabbed the paddle and tossed the rope into the ancient canoe.

"Sure! I'm not a dope!" Mackenzie snapped. She pulled off her shoes, tiptoed daintily to the boat, and plunked herself in, almost tipping the whole shebang into the murky water. The color drained from her cheeks and she gripped the sides of the canoe so hard her knuckles turned yellow. I pushed the canoe a little, kicked off, and swung my legs carefully around and in, placing myself in a comfy position. Mackenzie turned and stared at me. I swung out the paddle and heaved. Swing, dip, pull, glide, up; swing, dip, pull, glide, up....

Soon we were slowly and peacefully gliding across the water. "You want to paddle?" I asked Mackenzie.

"Uh, I don't feel like it," she said.

My arms were sore already. My hair was tucked under my backside, so it wouldn't go in the water. I strained and pulled.

After an uncomfortable silence Mackenzie (I'm going to just write Mack. I'm tired of writing her whole name.) broke it by saying uneasily, "I hear there's an island on this lake. A tiny one, but I hear it's cool."

"Unh," I grunted. There's not much to say when your arms are trying to paddle against gunky water.

"Look!" Mack cried, pointing ahead of us. I squinted into the sun. Yes! A green lump. Half gray. It had to be the island.

I pulled the paddle one more time and WOOSH! We were on the rocky shore of a little island. I flexed my arms. Sore as anything. I gingerly hopped out and tied the rope around a boulder. Mack cautiously threw her legs over the side. Bad idea! The canoe toppled over and she catapulted into the lake. SPLASH! Mack surfaced, spluttering and thrashing her arms crazily.

"Don't you know how to get out of a canoe?" I said, trying hard not to laugh.

Mack was a bunch of malarkey. "Yes, I do!" she squeaked. She crawled on shore. She looked like a drowned rat. Her wispy hair was frizzed and plastered to her skull, the curls turning into dreadlocks and snaggles. Her clothes were stuck to her body and makeup streaked her face in dark watery marks. Algae clung to her, like a green curtain. Mack stood up and pulled green off her jeans indignantly.

"C'mon. Let's go to the top of the island after we look around. You'll dry out quicker in the sun." Mack sure looked green around the gills. I chortled behind my cupped hand, almost keeling over, almost tripping over my hair. White lies. Mack definitely did not know how to canoe. I rubbed my sore arms and climbed up the rocks. We were even.

31 De Gabriella
Cappuccino Island

Diary,

We climbed up the little craggy hill until we got to soft grass. We stopped to catch our breath. Mack was picking on a scab. Yech! I think picking scabs is gross. They get all bloody and pink and infected, and then you end up with a permanent scar. Her skin had green bits flaking off it, with a few strands of algae still in her stiff hair.

Here are some calculations: The island is about twenty-six feet wide. The top of the hill is a bit narrower than the bottom, and there are twenty paces of shore at least. It's about one hundred feet long, up and down.

★ ★ ★

When we reached the top of the island I felt tri-
umphant. All sorts of bushes and big droopy trees
grow up there, and there's even a tiny natural pool.

"Let's explore the other side," I suggested.

Mack shook her head and whined, "I want to
dry off up here and clean up. I'll sit by this pool."
She firmly plopped onto the ground, emphasizing
that she wanted to stay.

I shrugged. Deity. What a powder puff. "I'm
going down. I'll be back," I carefully hiked down
the hill. There was all this black stone on the way
down. It could've been obsidian. Indians made
arrowheads out of obsidian. Toward the bottom I
noticed two slabs of the black stone. The hill caved
into a cozy cave, not very big, just large enough for
one person and a few possessions. The walls were of
grass and when I crawled inside, ferns fell like a
waterfall over the stone entrance. It was a great
place. It reminded me of the magnolia bush. I also
noticed in a musty corner a bunch of burlap bags.
Yuch! Were they stinky! I wanted to retch from the
smell. I also found a can of pork 'n' beans, a moldy
pack of bubble gum with only one piece left, and a
water-logged piece of paper that looked like a pretend treasure map. Cccoooooooooolllllllll!! (Now I
sound like Mouse.) It looked like somebody had

spent some time here on the island. I'd spend time here. I liked the island more than our cottage.

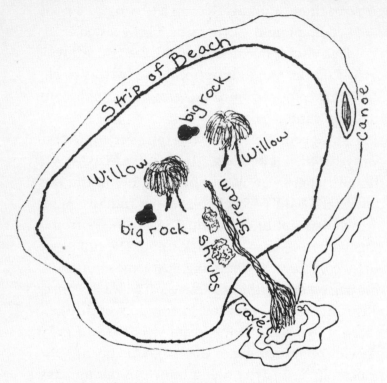

I hiked back up to Mack. Now my feet were sore, but I had made a discovery.

"This place is cool," Mack agreed. "Let's call it the De Gabriella Cappuccino Island."

32 Good-bye, So Soon

Diary,

Sorry, Mrs. Prince. I've been hanging out with Mack too much to write a lot.

Dad was ready to leave.

I really didn't want to go home that bad, but I guess I had to. I didn't mind my ugly room, the gross lake, or Mackenzie. We finally told each other we had lied. Her dad had really come up here to think about the divorce he had gone through recently, and he worked at a supermarket while Mack's mom was rich.

Benny and Yo-Yo wanted to go home and sign up for Little League.

I was going to miss the island. Deity. Now I sound all soft and mushy. But I wanted to see Jason, Iris, and Austen, but I couldn't decide who I wanted to see more. I slowly packed. My magnolia blossom had crumbled. And then I remembered the notes. I wondered if there were any more waiting for me in the magnolia bush. Suddenly I couldn't wait to get home, even if Mouse would be there, drooling over Austen and talking about Revlon in her turd-green and puke-yellow bathing suit.

33 Welcome Home!!

Diary,

We were surprised when we arrived home and found half the neighborhood in front of our house with a card table with a crystal bowl of red punch, a huge watermelon cut in half, hot dogs, hamburgers, fried chicken (cholesterol!), and a huge banner across our front door that said in bold red letters: WELCOME HOME!!

Mary Ellis, Susie, Iris, Jason, Mouse (who of course invited Austen), and Aunt Cathy were there. Deity! They were acting like we had been gone for decades!

Jason looked so cute! Even in an ordinary blue t-shirt, ripped-up jeans, and a floppy black fishing hat.

Iris was in a soft pink cardigan, low-cut cutoffs with embroidered flowers, and leather huaraches on her long, thin feet. It was so good to see her! I jumped out of the car and embraced her.

"Rapunzel! Long-time-no-see! Was wonderin'
when you would be back," Jason said.

I smiled.

Austen's face was a peculiar beet-red color. He
grinned, his hair shoved over his eyes.

Marjorie tugged on his arm and whispered in his
ear. She was wearing a blue tank top that showed
her still-peeling back, and green shorts.

"Pru! It's so good to see you! Your dream candle
is all ready! Oh, this is just so great!" Iris said. She
squeezed my hand.

"Hiiiiiiii, Pruuudeeence. My mom thought up
this party," Marjorie said, very smugly, grasping
Austen's arm. She was even shorter than he was! Her
hair was fluffed out behind her head and she had
bangs now.

Aunt Cathy grabbed me and squeezed me so
tight and hard I thought my ribs would crack. She's
Mom's sister and her hair is dark brown and her
eyes are sharp hazel, like Mom's. They're practically
twins—just two years apart.

"Aunt Cathy! What are you doing here!?" I
exclaimed. Yeah, why was she there? She said she
liked the nudist colony in all of her letters. Her eyes
sparkled brightly. She squeezed my shoulders and a

smile teased upon her lips. "Later," she whispered as if we shared a big secret.

Ugh! I hate being in suspense! I was itching to check if I had received any more notes. "Uh, Iris, help me unpack," I muttered. I hadn't told her about the notes yet and I was just dying to.

She bobbed her head, then pointed at her teeth. Clean, perfectly square, and sparkling white.

"Wow! You got your braces off! I totally forgot! They look fantastic! Let's go." I flashed Jason (sigh) a smile and tugged Iris on the arm. We ran.

34 Notes and Fried Chicken

Diary,

I told Iris about the notes.

"Ooooh! A secret admirer! Oh please let's go look in the magnolia bush!" Iris cried. Then she paused. "Have you told Marj?" she asked. I shook my head and Iris clasped her hands together. "Oh boy! A real secret!"

★ ★ ★

We pranced (literally) out into the backyard. It looked the same. Bush, oak tree, sandbox, swings. We went to the magnolia bush. The closer we got, the more blue and white slips of paper we saw. We snatched them off in bunches and crawled under the bush.

I uncovered my stuff. Dry. A bunch of ants were

attacking the old V-8. I threw the can out onto the lawn and wiped off my fingers.

I cleared my throat and held up the first note.

Whoever is happy will make others happy too.
—Anne Frank

Just then, Marjorie ducked into the bush. I stuffed the notes behind an orange crate.

"C'mon, let's eat," she said.

Iris and I gave each other a private look and went to go have fried chicken. I'm not going to write Mither about this party!

35 The Deep, Dark Secret of Cathy Sunfellow

Diary,

Aunt Cathy looked pretty in a bright blue gingham dress with a matching blue belt, a blue bow, and blue high heels. She was also wearing the locket Uncle Dan gave her for Christmas. Blush was brushed onto her high cheekbones and green eye shadow was brushed on her lids, lightly. I was surprised she wasn't wearing her feather boa. It was after supper. Aunt Cathy was spending a week with us. She hadn't eaten.

"Well?" I questioned with my eyes. Mom and Dad and the boys were watching a rerun of <u>Leave It to Beaver</u> in the den.

Aunt Cathy's big hands closed around mine and she led me into the kitchen. While she made herbal tea and stared out the window, she told me her secret. She had responded to an ad in the Young

Lovers section of the newspaper. She was going to meet a man tonight for supper. He lived in town, so she had left the nudist colony to meet him. His name was Brit—Brit Benson.

"So is this some sort of blind date?" I asked.

Aunt Cathy laughed. She tapped her magenta nails on the table, making a clicking sound. She took a sip of tea and shrugged.

"Here. This is Brit's ad. My kind of guy, but he's late," Aunt Cathy said. She handed me the ad, torn from the newspaper. I grabbed it excitedly. It read:

40+ Man, Looking For True Love
Six-foot-two, retired skier. My current interest is astronomy and I work as a substitute English teacher. I love fun, travel, reading by a cozy fire, family reunions. I am a health nut. I enjoy growing things and private times. I am looking for a long term relationship. Let's talk, I want to know you. Phone: 555-4888.

"Oooohh...," I crooned. A smile crept over my face. I sighed. "I'm in the mood for loooooove," I sang in a high voice.

Aunt Cathy laughed and gave me a playful slap. The doorbell rang and she froze. "Aaahh...," she said. I nodded and gestured for her to open the door. She slowly stood up and floated to the door.

"Camille!" I heard a deep voice rumble. Aunt Cathy's real name is Camille, but she usually prefers Cathy, I think because when she was a teen everyone called her Chamomile Tea.

"Brit? Good to meet you," I heard Aunt Cathy say. "Come in. This is my sister's home."

A big, thin man came in. He had on jeans, boots, a leather jacket, and his long gray hair was pulled into a ponytail.

"Ah, and who is this lovely lady?" Brit asked, smiling at me. He had a motorcycle helmet tucked under his arm.

"My niece, Prudence. Prudence, this is my friend, Mr. Brit Benson," Aunt Cathy said formally. She gave me a dreamy smile. I grinned, glad she was happy. Brit shook my hand. His cologne wafted around the kitchen. Old Spice.

"Off to dinner. Then a concert. Good-bye, Prudence, nice to meet you," Brit said.

Aunt Cathy and Brit went out the door, their laughter floating away with them.

36 Mouse's Breakdown

Diary,

"Love is feared, but rules all," I read to Iris.

"Romantic...but what does it mean?" she said.

We were up in my room. I shrugged and toyed with my dream candle.

The door burst open and Mouse stood there, breathless, red in the face, her hair in wild tufts. "Well, (puff, puff) your Aunt Cathy (puff, puff) is whew! I saw your aunt with a guy!" she said.

I shrugged. "So? That's Brit. Mooooooom!" I said, shouting at the end.

"Yes, Chickabiddy Baby?" she called up to me. She was with Susie and Mary Ellis, baking molasses cookies.

"Have you met Brit?" I yelled.

"Yup" was the reply.

Mouse slammed the door and broke down in a heap on the floor.

I leaned over the edge of my bed to get a better look. "What is it, Marjorie? What's wrong?" I asked.

Her shoulders shook with heavy sobs and her tears spattered onto my light purple carpet. My whole room is mostly purple, which used to be my favorite color in second grade. Now my favorite colors are dark blue and wine-red.

Mouse just kept sobbing.

Iris leaned expectantly over the side of the bed.

Mouse finally stopped crying and told us the five major problems of her life:

1. Her mother (Mary Ellis) didn't like Austen at all.
2. Austen had just dumped her today.
3. Her dad wouldn't be back from Sacramento until late December.
4. She had to learn flute and then go to a music camp.
5. She had the positive signs of acne.

I patted her back awkwardly. "It's okay."

Iris passed us a handful of Kleenex and Mouse blew her nose several times. Then she added in a small, forced voice that quivered, "And you aren't my friend anymore...just Iris's best friend."

"Well," I explained carefully, "it's just that you were acting like such a snot." Mouse threw her arms around me and started bawling all over again. She squeezed me tight which made the bumps on my chest hurt like crazy. I rolled my eyes at Iris. Then Mouse said in choked sobs, "And Jason...he just likes you!" She suddenly stood up and bolted out the door.

I turned to Iris.

"She is <u>good</u>! Jason does like you!" she said.

I practically fainted. I sucked in a giant breath. "Is he the one who is sending all those notes to me?"

Iris just shrugged and I could finally breathe normally again.

37 Mega Love

Diary,

Iris and I have been counting the days until we go to Fairview Middle School. It's late July, nearly July the thirtieth. We have until September fourth to become fifth graders. The big five.

(Well, Mrs. Prince, this is my fourth little blue notebook. I bet you're itching to find out who has been sending me all those notes, huh? Well you're about to find out....)

★ ★ ★

Iris and I were in her room, playing Trivial Pursuit, listening to Jason's Purple Devils CD that he was booming all over the house:

"Mega llooooove! Boom, boom, bah, boon, ba-ba! You are myah meg-ga love! Boom, bah, bah, boon ba-bah boom!

"Yellow hair, big blue eyes, ya broke my hear-rrt, right in half! Boom-boom, bah!

"Tears in my ey-eyes, wretched meg-ga lo-ove! Break my heart. Tears from my eyes, on ya sweatah! Keep away from me, ya you bettah...or I might love ya, love ya, mega looove! Boom-boom bah! Boom ba-ba! Meg-ga-ga, gonna be my meeeeegggggggaaaaa looooove! Ya so fine and pretty, while I'm so BEEP...."

"Why did the song beep?" I asked Iris.

"Bad word, rhymes with pretty," Iris said.

I nodded and rolled the dice. Jason's music shook and rocked the walls. I wondered if I was Jason's mega love. "When are you going to have your party?" I asked Iris. For some reason I had just remembered it.

"Well, it was going to be this August, but mom wants it to be in October. Doesn't that stink?" Iris grumbled.

"Meeeeegah! Ya my girl! Be my girl! I love ya, babe! Boom-boom, ba, ba boom-boom bah!

"Mega, mega loove! Mega lloooooove, oh yeah! Be myah mega love! Ya so pretty while I'm so BEEP! Boom, bah-bah!

"Can't ya see, I love ya! Megggaaaah! Oh yeah! Plleeeeaaazzze be myah megah love! Ya walkin' along, ya look so pretty, ah doo wa ditty! How ya been doin'? I'm just fine. Will you be mine!? Mega love! Boom-boom bah, bah boom bah-bah!

"Ya myah girl! Babe, ya myah mega love!"

The door burst open and Jason sidled in, wearing baggy black pants with a silver wallet chain dangling down, a tight baseball sweatshirt and his black fishing hat tipped at an angle on his head so his thick blonde curls matted across his forehead. He was holding a can of purple grape pop in his hand.

"Rapunzel, Little Sis, be my mega love, heh, heh. Who's winnin'?" He plopped down next to me.

"Pru. She has four pieces of her pie filled up," Iris said.

"Yummyyyy. What's your favorite pie, Rapunzel?" Jason said. He was so cute! The electric sparks bounced around in the pit of my stomach.

"Blackberry. I think it's the best," I said.

"Yummers! It's my mega love," Jason laughed and took a swig of his soda.

"Jason, would you kindly get out of my room and quit flirting with my friend!" Iris said crisply.

"Okay, Little Sis...take it eeeaaaassyyyyy," Jason said.

I gave Iris a dirty look as Jason slid off the bed.

He swaggered out, saying over the blare of his obnoxious music, "Kindly walk, do not run, to the nearest exit."

And then I looked out the window. And gasped. And rubbed my eyes. And then looked out the window again. And groaned.

Austen Russel was putting a note on my magnolia bush!!

I screamed and fell off the bed. Literally.

38 The Discovered Lover

Diary,

I galloped down the stairs with Iris chasing after me and screaming, "Wait! What is it?! Hey, Pruuuu!"

I couldn't stop. Oh why couldn't it have been Jason? His song was booming all over the house. I streaked through the kitchen past Ms. Gray.

"Prudence!? What the—?" she yelled.

I leaped off the front porch and bounded across the street. I clawed up my fence and scrambled over the honeysuckle bushes. Austen saw me coming and started running around the back of the house. He jumped the fence. I ran and jumped over it too. I ran down the street after him, my feet pounding on the asphalt.

"Wait! Stop! Stop!" I jumped with all my might and tackled him, pushing him onto the ground. My hair whipped my cheeks and I skinned my knees crashing onto the sidewalk in front of Mouse's house. I rolled off him and onto Mouse's front lawn, narrowly missing the sprinklers.

Iris jogged up. "Ah. A discovered lover. L'amour!" she sighed.

"Deity!" I said, loudly.

Austen scrambled up, found that nobody was chasing him anymore and ran off, not even asking if I was okay.

Suddenly the screen door to Mouse's house burst open and Mouse flew out. "Austen—?!" she called.

"Well, was he sending the notes, Pru? Huh, didja find out?" Iris asked me, tugging on my arm and pulling me up to my feet.

I pretended I didn't hear her and examined my scratched up legs and my skinned, bleeding knees.

But Mouse heard. Oh boy did she hear! "What notes!?" she demanded, her hands on her knobby hips. Her hair flew out in all directions. She side-stepped the sprinklers and came up to me and Iris. "Austen...sent you notes?" she whispered.

I just closed my eyes.

"Austen sent you notes!?" Mouse repeated, but this time she screeched.

"Iris," I said through gritted teeth.

39 Fed Up!!

Diary,

I sipped my raspberry Italian soda. We were at FlavorBest. Me, Mouse, and Iris.

I had to explain the whole shebang to Mouse. She was drinking a Blueberry Frost, her eyes were all red and puffy. Silent sobs shook her shoulders. "I knew he liked you," she half-squeaked, half-whimpered.

Iris gave me a look and gulped down half her Orange Tangy-Spice.

I wasn't sure if I should laugh or cry. I didn't know if I liked Austen as much as I liked Jason, or vice versa. It was all so complicated!

"Mouse, er, Marjorie, don't take it so hard. You're only, uh, er, ten," I said.

"Yeah, and you're eleven! Everybody likes you!" Mascara and blush muddied her face as tears dripped all the way down her neck.

"Anything wrong, Sweetie-Pie?" The waitress asked Mouse in a high, nasal voice.

"No!" Mouse snapped.

"We're just fine," Iris said quietly.

The waitress shook her head and stalked away muttering something that sounded like "Kids these days! No manners at all."

I glanced out the window and saw Aunt Cathy and Brit zoom away on Brit's motorcycle. I smiled at them, even though I knew they couldn't see me.

"This is not funny!" Mouse said, poking out her lower lip.

I let out a breath, slowly sucked it back in, and counted to ten inside my head. I read in <u>Young Psychology News</u> magazine, while I was waiting in the dentist's office, that if you hold your breath and count slowly to ten, or even better, twenty, you are more likely not to lose your cool. It's supposed to bring patience and understanding to the brain. I felt like quoting Rhett Butler in <u>Gone with the Wind</u> to Mouse. I was just sick of her outbursts.

I slurped up the rest of my Italian soda and watched Mouse start on a fresh new batch of exaggerated tears. She was always trying to get all the attention! I was just so fed up!!

"Well? Say something!" Mouse sobbed. So I did.

"Frankly, Mouse, I don't give a damn!" I yelled, slamming my fist on the table. I ran out of that FlavorBest and raced down the street for home.

40 Too Much News

Diary,

Little Women

Chapter 28: Very good!

Quilt Records

Finally we are actually sewing it together!

I got this note on my magnolia bush today:

A friend is a present you give yourself.—R.L.S.

I didn't catch Austen.

(Dad read all of the notes I have received so far and typed them all up. He's calling this book A Warp in Time.)

I actually got two notes today. The other one was a Nigerian proverb. It said:

Hold a true friend with your hands.

Today the ball dropped. The world stopped turning. My heart stopped beating. (Okay, okay, I'll get to the point.) Today Iris told me that Jason had hired Austen to deliver all those notes to me. She hadn't told me because now Jason liked a fifteen-year-old and they were going to go out on a date next Friday.

I am about ready to tear everyone's hair clear out of their heads because:

1. Benny and Yo-yo wouldn't stop raving about the Mets game they saw and how fabulous it was.
2. Mom and Dad won't stop acting all lovey-dovey.
3. Mouse is not speaking to me. (Not that I care very much at all.)
4. I am not speaking to Mouse, Jason, Austen, or Iris.
5. Aunt Cathy is constantly raving about Brit Benson.

Brit is going to come over for dinner. So of course Aunt Cathy insisted on cooking for what she called a "special occasion." She's going to make pasta, veal, mashed potatoes, and fruit salad.

The boys are spending the night at someone's house again.

Brit came over at around six or six-thirty. His gray hair was brushed out over his broad shoulders. He was wearing tight (very tight) suede pants with gold buttons going up their sides, a paisley shirt open at the neck (ew!) and a red scarf around his neck, a jean jacket, and a thick gold chain. He did not seem like Aunt Cathy's type at all, but I guess that wasn't for me to determine. Guess what, now Aunt Cathy is writing a new book called <u>Happily Ever After: How to Find the Perfect Gal or Guy</u>.

Pathetic! Malarkey! She was on cloud nine, in seventh heaven.

I hated Jason so much! I scowled when I heard his music booming across the street:

"Mega love! Babe, ya myah mega love! Boom-boom, bo bopbipettey! Bah-bah! Mega love...."

"There's something we need to tell," Brit said, smiling and taking Aunt Cathy's hand in his.

41 An Announcement

Diary,

"Camille and I have decided that we love each other very, very much. We are engaged."

I gasped and a glob of mashed potatoes fell out of my mouth and back onto my plate. "Deity," I murmured. "Holy Toledo!" I shouted.

Mom was crying crazily, dabbing at her face with a napkin. Dad kept slapping his thigh and saying, "Well, how about that!" And of all things, Aunt Cathy and Brit were French kissing!

I scooped and shoveled food into my mouth. What was there to say? Yuck! Aunt Cathy was not a good cook. What would Brit do? The veal Aunt Cathy had made was overcooked and tasted like salted cardboard, the mashed potatoes still had the potato skins in them, the pasta was brown at the edges, and the fruit salad had orange peels and watermelon rinds accompanying the too tart or too rotten fruit. But I ate. And ate. My stomach and tastebuds seemed to be numb.

The doorbell rang. Saved by the bell! I jumped up, scraping back my chair so hard that it fell over. I mumbled some excuse and padded in my socks to the front door. I opened it slowly.

Austen stood there in the doorway.

I felt even sicker than when Brit announced the engagement.

"Hey there, Pudding-Head," Austen said, smiling that smile of his.

I swallowed the last of my mashed potatos and veal, and just mumbled under my breath, "Deity...."

"Oh, Chickie Baby! You've got a little friend! That is just so sweet!" Mom called to me, smiling and leaning back in her chair so she could see Austen better.

I stepped outside and quickly closed the door. "Yeah?" I asked Austen. I was sweating horribly in my sweater, even though it was pretty cool outside, and my hair felt like an anvil, weighing me down. This had happened before, at the 7-11. Oh, boy. I stared at the tiny replica of myself, deep in Austen's pupils.

"Well...what I'm trying to tell you is...that I like

you," Austen muttered, shuffling his feet and looking down, so my reflection in his eyes shattered.

"I guess you're...okay too," I whispered.

From across the street, Jason's stupid Purple Devils CD swallowed up my words:

"Megaaaa loove! Oh, yeah! Pretty, pretty, pretty, and you're all mine! Boom-boom bah, bippety boppitey bah!

"Mega love...."

Before I knew what was happening at all, Austen laid a soft, light kiss on my lips. His eyes were closed, and his breath smelled like he had just brushed his teeth. He had definitely planned this. It felt...nice. But I pulled back inside and slammed the door in Austen's face. What could I do? What could I say? I pulled the door open and kissed Austen's sunburned lips quickly back, and then slammed the door in his face again.

42 See Ya!

Diary,

<u>Little Women</u>

Chapter 47: I enjoyed this book very much.
But boy was it hard to follow! I wish I could
write a book as good as <u>Little Women</u>, but
alas, no. Do I ever recommend this book!

Quilt Records
We are all done!!! And boy is it beautiful!
Mom will enter it in the fair that is coming up,
but after that it stays with us, hanging in the
living room.

I absolutely, positively LOVED this summer!
Even fights with Mouse, heartbreaks, hangovers,
bad puns, wacky hormones, notes, the cottage,
Mither, and white lies. It was the best summer I've
ever had. Even non-sensible and action packed.

★ ★ ★

Yo, Mrs. Prince, are you proud of me? Are you just wriggling to tell the other teachers all my secrets?

Now I am saving up money from baby-sitting, pet-sitting, and mowing people's lawns for a computer. So the next time you assign summer diaries I won't get any calluses from writing with a pencil!

School has started and I'm ready for it! The principal gave me permission to do a school newspaper. Iris, Mouse, and Austen help out a lot.

The Fairview Middle School Gazette

Columns

School Secrets	
Dear Aunt Camille	1
A Note from the Principal	2
School News & Events	3
Moola!!	3
Neighborly News	4
Jokes, Riddles, Games & Fun!	4
	5

School Secrets by Marjorie Ann Jenkins

(Names are changed to protect other people's feelings.)

♥ Louisa loves baseball player number 28!!!

† Shhhh... One teacher has a mug that says G-O-D.

♥ Bob loves Rachel. They kissed and Bob sent notes to Rachel!

If you have any secrets that you would like to share, just write!

DEAR AUNT CAMILLE

Is your love life rotten?
Do your parents stink?
Do you need to get money fast?
Write to Aunt Camille!
Letters & Answers
by Prudence Brinker

Dear Aunt Camille,
I love this really cute boy! How can I get him to notice me?
--A Desperate Lover!

**Dear Desperate Lover,
Join clubs he's in! Say hi every morning. Call him up and ask for assignments you missed. Act friendly.
Good Luck!
--Aunt Camille**

****

Dear Aunt Camille,
My grandparents drive me nuts! They buy me baby presents and never let me see PG-13 movies. I'm fourteen! Please help!
--Fed Up!

**Dear Fed Up,
Try gently talking out your feelings with your nutty grandparents. Tell them you feel trapped.
Good Luck!
--Aunt Camille**

A Note from the Principal

Dear Students,

Welcome to Fairview Middle School. We hope you enjoy your stay here until eighth grade. I want to commend the wonderful work Iris, Prudence, Austen, and Marjorie have done on our newspaper, <u>The Fairview Middle School Gazette</u>.

Many thanks,

Mr. Newton

SCHOOL NEWS & EVENTS

by Austen Russell

The school is receiving a great new goal for the soccer field, and a new dome and swing sets! HOORAY FOR FAIRVIEW!!!

Halloween Dance (costumes required)   October 15th
Thanksgiving Feast   November 15th
December Dance   December 10th
Papier-Mâché Classes   January 8th–12th
Sixth Grade Dance   February 3rd
Spring Dance   April 4th
Soccer Sign-ups   May 5th
Eighth Grade Pre-tour   June 10th
I hope you can join us!!!

$ $ MOOLA!!

by Prudence Brinker & Iris Gray

Ways to get money—fast!

• Make cookies (at least two different kinds) and lemonade. Load it up on a tray or in a wagon and sell it around the block.

• Set up a car wash or lemonade stand.

• Put up baby-sitting ads.

• Have a garage sale or yard sale.

HAVE IDEAS? SHARE THEM!

Neighborly News

by Austen & Marjorie & Prudence & Iris

Mrs. Mary Ellis Jenkins is having an addition to Pepperfarm Lane—A BABY! WELCOME!

Leelo Perkins just learned how to ride his bike! GOOD JOB!

Susie Gray got a job as a successful quilter and painter. Thanks, Susie, for all your hard work and big efforts!

On Ornate Street they are building a brand new mansion! Let's hope a nice family moves in—maybe a rock band!

Jokes, Riddles, Games & FUN!

When does a dollar bill have antlers?
When it's a buck! Chortle!

Unscramble these words!
sejok
didlres
mesga
NFU

FUN
games
riddles
jokes

Rub your tummy and pat your head at the same time! It might sound easy.... Try it!!

From Little Women,
last chapter, last sentence:
"Oh, my girls, however long you may live,
I never can wish you a greater happincss
than this!"

123

A Note from the Publisher

If you enjoyed reading *The Diary of Chickabiddy Baby*,
we'd like to hear from you. Please send us your thoughts
(don't forget your name and address), and we'll send you
a Chickabiddy postcard. Thanks!

Tricycle Press
P.O. Box 7123
Berkeley, CA 94707